THE ADVENTURES OF
BATGIRL
AND
SUPERGIRL

THE CITY-WIDE SCREAM SCHEME

BY JAY ALBEE
ILLUSTRATED BY TEO DUARTE

BATGIRL CREATED BY BOB KANE WITH BILL FINGER
SUPERGIRL BASED ON CHARACTERS CREATED BY JERRY SIEGEL AND JOE SHUSTER
BY SPECIAL ARRANGEMENT WITH THE JERRY SIEGEL FAMILY

raintree
a Capstone company — publishe

T0372157

Raintree is an imprint of Capstone Global Library Limited, a company
incorporated in England and Wales having its registered office at 264
Banbury Road, Oxford, OX2 7DY – Registered company number: 6695582

www.raintree.co.uk
myorders@raintree.co.uk

Designed by Hilary Wacholz
Originated by Capstone Global Library Ltd

978 1 3982 5310 0

British Library Cataloguing in Publication Data
A full catalogue record for this book is available from the British Library.

Printed and bound in India.

CONTENTS

MEET . . .

BATGIRL

REAL NAME: Barbara Gordon

BASE: Gotham City

Barbara is the daughter of Police Commissioner James Gordon. She created her own Batsuit and joined the Batman Family without her father's knowledge. Using her brilliant mind, talent for tech and mastery of martial arts, she cracks down on crime.

SUPERGIRL

REAL NAME: Kara Zor-El

BASE: Metropolis

Kara escaped from her doomed home planet, Krypton, before it exploded. She and her cousin, Superman, now protect their adopted home, Earth. The planet's yellow sun gives her incredible superpowers that she uses to take down the fiercest foes.

Now, the courageous girls
are teaming up to fight for
all that's good and right.
These are . . .

THE ADVENTURES OF
BATGIRL
AND
SUPERGIRL

Chapter 1

MUSEUM MYSTERY

ZIIIP!

Batgirl's grapnel neatly caught the shining spire of a skyscraper. She flipped and swooped through Metropolis, on her way to meet her friend Supergirl. At the top of her next flip, Batgirl activated her cape's glider mode. The fluttering cape snapped stiff and caught the air. She sailed gracefully between the tall buildings.

"I'm nearly at the museum," Batgirl said into her earpiece.

"I know," replied Supergirl with a laugh. "I'm right behind you!"

Batgirl looked over her shoulder and saw Supergirl flying casually alongside her. "Oh, hey!"

Supergirl waved and Batgirl grinned. Together the two friends glided high above the city streets.

"It's a beautiful day," said Supergirl, squinting in the late afternoon sun. "Are you sure you wouldn't rather go to the beach?"

"Are you kidding?!" Batgirl replied. "We're getting a private, sneak-peek tour of the Metropolis Museum's rare book exhibit! What could be better than that?"

Supergirl chuckled. "You are *such* a book nerd."

"Yeah, I am!" Batgirl agreed. "I'm just glad we were able to save so many of those beauties from that warehouse fire last week. When we get to the museum, you'll appreciate how amazing they are."

"I don't think books are that exciting. But I *am* looking forward to checking out the fossils," said Supergirl. "I love Earth animals."

"Didn't you have, like, flashbirds and fish-snakes on Krypton?" asked Batgirl.

"Sure," replied Supergirl. "But have you *seen* a trilobite? Those things are wild."

Batgirl and Supergirl landed on the front steps of the Metropolis Museum. The building's marble columns reached high above them. A banner fluttered between two of the columns. It read, "OPENING TOMORROW! ANCIENT BOOKS OF THE WORLD."

The museum had just closed for the day. The last visitors trotted down the steps past the Super Heroes. A few stopped for selfies.

SKREEEEEEEEEEEEEE

Supergirl froze mid-step, and her eyes went wide. Her super-hearing had caught a weird, wild sound coming from inside the museum. "Something's wrong!" she said.

Batgirl snapped into action mode. She turned to the people on the steps. "Everybody, get clear! Quick!"

The visitors dashed away. At the same time, Batgirl and Supergirl charged forward into the museum. The grand entrance hall was empty.

"What is it?" Batgirl asked her teammate.

"I heard a strange sound. Like a monstrous scream," Supergirl replied. "It's stopped. But it came from this way."

The pair ran through the medieval armour collection. They hurried past ancient Egyptian statues. Then they dashed into the rare book exhibit.

They found security guards and museum staff lying on the floor, groggy and stunned. The people were holding their heads and ears. Something had clearly happened. But the room looked oddly untouched.

WHOOSH! WHOOSH!

At super-speed, Supergirl rushed around the exhibit. She checked people for injuries. Everyone was dazed but okay. She started easing them into seated positions.

As Supergirl zipped among the staff, Batgirl spotted the rare books curator. "Joan!" she said, running over. Joan groaned as Batgirl helped her sit up. "What happened?"

Joan shook her head. "I–I don't know. I heard this ear-splitting wail. It was like a siren, but also not like a siren at all. I've never heard anything like it. Next thing I knew, you were helping me up."

"I saw it," said a security guard sitting nearby. His face was pale. "The thing that made that . . . noise. It had bone white hair and a face like a skull. It was a *ghost.*"

"A ghost?" asked Batgirl. "What would a ghost want with rare books?"

Joan gasped. "Oh no! The books!" She stumbled to her feet and ran clumsily, but as quickly as she could, between the display cases. She took stock of the exhibit items.

"Only one book is missing," Joan said. She stopped next to a broken, empty case. Batgirl and Supergirl came up beside her.

Joan looked around again. "I don't get it. The missing book is an ancient tome of lore and spell craft. It isn't very valuable. Some of the other books in the exhibit are priceless. So why take this one?"

Batgirl frowned in thought. What a mystery.

WHOOP! WHOOP!

Joan and other staff flinched at the sudden sound. Supergirl checked a small watch she wore under her glove.

"Looks like there's more trouble! I've just received a red alert from the S.T.A.R. Labs compound," Supergirl said.

Batgirl's frown deepened. S.T.A.R. Labs was the most high-tech scientific research facility in the world. It was also one of the most secure compounds in the area. Red alerts were extremely rare.

"Then we have to investigate," said Batgirl. "Will you be okay, Joan?"

"Yes, I'll be fine," the curator replied. "Go! Go!"

The Super Heroes turned on their heels and bolted for the door. Before they left, Batgirl called out, "I promise to get that book back, Joan!"

On the museum steps, Supergirl said, "We need to get to S.T.A.R. Labs fast. I'll give you a lift." She held Batgirl around the waist. "Brace yourself."

They launched straight up into the sky.

WHOOOOSH!

Buildings began rushing by in a blur. Batgirl squeezed her eyes shut. *Don't be sick, don't be sick,* she thought.

She knew that Supergirl wasn't flying at full power – faster than a speeding bullet. But it was still dizzying.

Instead of thinking about zooming at tremendous speeds over trees and fields, Batgirl wondered what they would find at S.T.A.R. Labs. Would it be the skull-faced ghost with the siren wail? Batgirl shuddered. They would know soon enough.

Chapter 2

KNOCKED OUT

The Super Heroes sped towards the emergency at S.T.A.R. Labs. Still a few miles away, Supergirl tried using her super-vision to check the situation.

"I can't see through the lead-reinforced outer walls," she reported to her teammate over their earpieces. "But I can hear a commotion inside."

A moment later, Supergirl and Batgirl landed outside the compound.

SMAAASH!

In the next second, a two-tonne hydro generator burst through the building's thick security wall! Supergirl and Batgirl leaped to the side as the machine flew past. It bounced a few times before skidding to a stop in the nearly empty car park.

"Someone must be having a bad day at the lab," said Supergirl.

Batgirl cautiously peered through the hole. *CRUMPLE! KER-CRASH!* She didn't need super-hearing to pick up the sounds of destruction coming from inside. "And they haven't finished yet," she added.

"I'll scout things out and make sure no one is in harm's way," said Supergirl. "If the intruder can do this kind of damage to a reinforced wall, we need to be careful."

Batgirl nodded. "I'll wait for your signal."

Supergirl swooped through the gaping hole. Only the outer walls were reinforced with lead, so she used her X-ray vision to search the torn-up compound for S.T.A.R. Labs staff. Fortunately, it was after normal working hours. There were very few people. But everyone she did find was unconscious.

"The scientists and security are knocked out, just like at the museum!" Supergirl told Batgirl over their earpieces. She checked for injuries and found nothing serious. She let out a sigh of relief. Some of these scientists were her friends. S.T.A.R. Labs often supported Super Heroes with their brand-new technologies, and Supergirl had worked with the staff many times before.

"Strange," Batgirl replied. "Any signs of what could be behind it?"

Supergirl turned in a circle, peering through every wall. She saw–

"Silver Banshee!" Supergirl exclaimed.

"Of course!" Batgirl said. "I've read about her in the Justice League database. White hair, skull-like face . . . She fits the creepy description from the museum security guard. She must have hit the museum too."

"She's doing more than that now," Supergirl said. "She's tearing the labs apart!"

CRRRUNCH!

With her X-ray vision, Supergirl watched Silver Banshee rip a reinforced steel door off its hinges like it was foil. The supernatural Super-Villain threw the door aside and stepped into the room. She tore open all the cupboards and every piece of equipment. Then she moved on to the next locked door.

"This isn't just a rampage," Supergirl realized. "I think she's looking for something but hasn't found it yet. She seems frustrated."

Standing in the wreckage of another destroyed lab, Silver Banshee punched clean through a concrete wall.

"Yep, definitely frustrated," confirmed Supergirl.

Batgirl crouched by the outer wall. She read the screen on her wrist computer. "Not much is known about Silver Banshee, but there are some details. She's super-strong. She's also super-fast. The most interesting thing is–"

As her teammate talked, Supergirl scanned ahead of Silver Banshee's position. In a lab, behind a locked door, the hero spotted a single scientist who was still awake. Supergirl recognized her instantly. "Vivian!"

Last summer, Vivian had helped Supergirl by developing tech to track a tricky shape-shifting alien. The scientist's lab was at the end of a long corridor. Silver Banshee was at the other end, moving closer, room by room.

Supergirl dashed through the maze-like building. She had to protect her scientist friend and confront the crook!

"Wait," urged Batgirl, "there's more! Don't get–"

But it was too late. Supergirl had caught up to Silver Banshee. "Stop right there!" the Girl of Steel commanded.

Silver Banshee hardly looked up from the security panel that she was ripping out of the wall.

SKREEEEEEEEEEEEEEEEEEEEEEEEEEE!

The Super-Villain let out a wail. Her mouth stretched unnaturally wide. The air shuddered with sonic shock waves.

Supergirl felt the scream inside every cell of her body. Her vision spiralled and then cut to black.

When Supergirl blinked her eyes again, she saw Batgirl crouched over her. The Girl of Steel's ears rang, and her brain felt like cotton.

Batgirl held a finger to her lips in a "shhh" motion. She jerked her head to the side, and Supergirl looked over.

RIP! TEAR! CRASH!

Silver Banshee was breaking into a room halfway down the corridor.

The crook had clearly not yet found whatever she was after. She had resumed her rampage. The heroes needed to be careful not to draw their foe's attention.

Batgirl helped up her unsteady friend. They slipped into the nearest broken-open room. Supergirl needed a moment to recover.

Inside the room, Batgirl said, "I didn't get to the part in the report about Silver Banshee's wail. It stuns anyone within earshot."

"Ugh, no kidding. I shouldn't have rushed in," Supergirl replied, rubbing her ears. "I'll remember not to tell her to 'stop right there' next time."

"Yeah, I don't think Banshee is the type to take orders." Batgirl peered around the wrecked lab. "Ooh," she breathed. "Look at the prototypes! The experiments!"

As her head cleared, Supergirl smiled at her friend's delight.

Batgirl grinned back. "I know, not just a book nerd! A tech nerd too!" She reached under a crushed desk and picked up a prototype stun gun. "This could come in handy in stopping our intruder. She's had a busy day, and whatever she's up to–"

"–it can't be good," finished Supergirl. She stood straight and rolled her shoulders back. She scanned the corridor with her X-ray vision. "Silver Banshee is almost to Vivian. Let's go and silence her racket!"

The pair dashed out from the room. Seconds later, Silver Banshee stomped into the corridor too. Her bottomless eyes immediately locked on to the heroes. She growled low and terrible.

Supergirl didn't flinch. She blasted her heat vision.

BFFFFZZZZZZZZT!

The fiery beams shot right at Silver Banshee . . . who dodged them! The Super-Villain was just as fast as Supergirl!

Silver Banshee scowled at the attack, her skull face twisting into something even more dreadful. She drew in a big breath. Again, Supergirl blasted her heat vision. Again, Silver Banshee dodged.

But this time, Batgirl was ready for the foe's countermove. She fired the stun gun.

ZZZERT!

A direct hit! The stun gun beam knocked Silver Banshee over. But it did not knock her *out*.

Batgirl looked down at the prototype, disappointed. "Not so stunning after all."

Silver Banshee muttered as she got to her feet, "My plans will not be foiled. No one will stop me. I am too close."

The Super Heroes didn't wait to hear any more. They unleashed everything they had at the Super-Villain.

Batgirl flung a Batarang. It flew towards Silver Banshee and burst open.

MMMPH!

Ice instantly coated Silver Banshee's mouth. Her scream was stifled!

Before Silver Banshee could react, Supergirl rushed forward with super-speed. She crashed her foe through a concrete wall.

SMASH!

Silver Banshee reeled. But the hard hit had also shattered the ice on her face.

SKRRRRRRREEEEEEEEEEEEEEEEEEE!

Silver Banshee screamed!

Supergirl was too close to avoid the blast!

The Girl of Steel caught the full force of the catastrophic sonic wave. Once again, the wail knocked her out cold.

Even from the other side of a concrete wall, Batgirl felt the indirect hit. Every bone in her body vibrated to Silver Banshee's wail. The walls swam around her as she sunk to the floor. Then her vision went dark.

Chapter 3

RESEARCH STATIONS

Batgirl came to with a screaming headache. Supergirl helped her to her feet.

"Are you okay?" Supergirl asked.

Batgirl nodded and immediately regretted it. It felt like her brain was bouncing around between her ringing ears.

"Do you think Silver Banshee even *has* an inside voice?" Batgirl asked, rubbing her head. "I'm guessing she got away? Did she take anything?"

"She did get away. My friend here can answer the second part. This is Vivian." Supergirl gestured to a woman in a lab coat, who smiled and waved hello. "Vivian is the head of research at S.T.A.R. Labs. She saw what happened after we were knocked out."

Supergirl helped Batgirl into the room at the end of the corridor – Vivian's lab. The scientist motioned the Super Heroes into her destroyed workspace.

"So," said Batgirl, "what happened? And how did you avoid the knockout wail?"

Vivian smiled and began signing.

Batgirl's eyes went wide. "Oh!" Vivian was deaf! That must have made her immune to Silver Banshee's sonic attack! Batgirl's mind tumbled this idea around. What could that mean for fighting their fierce foe?

"I saw Banshee on the security feed," signed Vivian. Supergirl translated for Batgirl. "It was clear her scream could knock people out. And when she started throwing around machinery and breaking walls, I knew I had to hide."

"I'm glad you did," said Supergirl.

Vivian nodded and continued. "After knocking you two out, she burst into my lab. She immediately started tearing it up. Moments later, the destruction stopped, and she was gone. Something else was gone too: a city-wide emergency broadcast system that I was developing."

Batgirl raised an eyebrow. "I read Lois Lane's *Daily Planet* article about that tech!" she said. "It's real next gen stuff. There was a public demonstration last week, right?"

Vivian nodded. "The problem with most emergency broadcast systems is that they are fixed in one place. They're vulnerable. A structure can get knocked down, power lines cut, or any number of things. My device can easily be connected to *any* transmission tower. I was working on the wireless uplink. For now, it has to be physically plugged in."

Vivian paused. She looked around her lab, reduced to rubble. "Silver Banshee destroyed so much just to get one piece of tech."

"She must be wanting to cause even more chaos," Supergirl said. "If Banshee can broadcast her wail city-wide, she could knock out *everyone*!"

"She could . . . ," agreed Batgirl. "But why would she? What advantage does that give her? And what's the rare book she stole from the museum got to do with it?"

BBAT BBAT

The console on Batgirl's wrist blinked with an incoming call. "It's Joan, the rare books curator," she said. She put the call on speaker, and Supergirl translated into sign for Vivian. "Joan, everything okay?"

"Batgirl, I've been looking into the book Silver Banshee stole. It's called the *Ghealach Grimoire*. *Ghealach* is Gaelic for *moon*. We had scans of the pages, and some of these spells seem pretty dangerous. There's alchemy, banishing, mind control–"

"Mind control!" Batgirl snapped her fingers. "That's it! Silver Banshee doesn't want to knock out everyone in Metropolis. She wants to enslave them! Her file said she has always had a thing for being in charge. A real hunger for power. But this is taking it to another level."

"Diabolical!" said Supergirl, Joan and Vivian at the same time.

"Vivian," said Batgirl, "how does the broadcast device achieve maximum reach?"

"The taller the broadcast antenna, the bigger the range," replied Vivian.

"Shuster Tower," said Supergirl. "That's got to be where Banshee is headed next. It's one of the tallest buildings in all Metropolis."

"One more thing," Joan said. "The book says the spell must be cast under a full moon."

Vivian signed urgently, "That's tonight!"

Batgirl tapped her wrist computer. "The moon rises in two hours. So we've got *some* time. Thanks for the info, Joan." Batgirl ended the call. She turned to Supergirl and Vivian. "We can't go at Silver Banshee head-on. We'll never get past her wail."

Vivian grinned. "I have an idea about that. Our security system records video *and* sound."

Batgirl immediately understood what the scientist was suggesting. "If we can make a sonic map of Silver Banshee's wail, maybe we can find a frequency that will neutralize it!"

"And we can make noise-cancelling earpieces that block out just that noise?" asked Supergirl.

Vivian nodded. She made two mirrored A-okay signs with her hands. "Exactly."

Vivian and Batgirl found a lab that was mostly undamaged. They cobbled together equipment, used a bashed up laptop to log in to the S.T.A.R. Labs security system, and then got to work.

Batgirl wasn't totally sure whether a recording of Silver Banshee's sonic blast would have the same effect as hearing it in person. She wasn't going to risk it, though. She kept the sound off.

Instead, Batgirl and Vivian looked over visual representations of the Super-Villain's powerful wail. Criss-crossing patterns slowly moved across their monitors.

"It's like no sonic signature I've ever seen." Vivian typed the words on a computer screen for Batgirl to read.

"Same," replied Batgirl. "This could take some time."

While Batgirl and Vivian twisted knobs and slid sliders, Supergirl helped the other S.T.A.R. Labs scientists recover from the attack.

With her super-speed, Supergirl cleared debris and rubble. *HEFT! HEAVE!* With her super-strength, she lifted twisted metal doors. *ZIP! ZOOM!*

With her invulnerability, Supergirl helped with more dangerous clean-up. One damaged prototype vibrated uncontrollably while blasting its laser. Supergirl wrestled the machine still so scientists could shut it off. Another experiment leaked radiation. Supergirl flew it into the sun. *BOOOOM!*

Later in the mostly undamaged lab, Vivian and Batgirl each let out heavy sighs. They had had little luck cracking Silver Banshee's sonic signature. They had written code to manipulate the sound pattern. They had stretched it, compressed it and turned it upside down. Every time they thought they had worked it out, they found something else new and baffling.

Another test had just failed. Frustrated, Vivian twisted an input knob harder than she meant. Batgirl saw the sonic map briefly flatten. She tapped Vivian on the shoulder.

"What was that? Do it again?" she asked.

Vivian twisted the knob once more. Her face lit up as she also saw the sonic map flatten out. They had found it – a counter frequency to neutralize Silver Banshee's wail!

"The aural temporal range!" Batgirl exclaimed. "Of course. You're brilliant, Vivian!"

Using the wrist computer in her Batsuit, Batgirl remotely hacked the earpieces she and Supergirl used to stay in contact. "I can jam the line open with this counter frequency. Then we should be able to hear each other but not get knocked out by that awful sound."

"You're pretty brilliant yourself!" said Vivian.

Batgirl finished the modifications and then tapped her earpiece. "Come in, Supergirl. Where are you?"

"Just on my way back from the sun," the Girl of Steel replied. "The light is fading fast over Metropolis. How's the science project coming along?"

"We cracked it!" Batgirl announced. "We can take on Silver Banshee now!"

"Good! That loudmouth villain thinks she can just waltz in and mind control the citizens of Metropolis without a fight. But . . ." There was burst of wind, and Supergirl was suddenly standing beside them in the lab. ". . . when she sees us again, she'll be singing a different tune."

Chapter 4

BATTLE FOR METROPOLIS

WHOOOOSH!

After waving goodbye to Vivian and with minutes to go before moonrise, Supergirl held on to Batgirl and rocketed them up into the sky. Batgirl squeezed her eyes closed and tried to ignore the sound of rushing wind.

"There!" called Supergirl. "I see Silver Banshee!"

Batgirl could hear her partner loud and clear over the earpiece. Batgirl opened her eyes . . . and then shut them tight again. Supergirl was using her super-vision to see far beyond normal human range. All Batgirl saw was the last of the sunset dissolving as Metropolis rushed towards them.

"We were right," Supergirl continued. "Silver Banshee is on Shuster Tower. She's plugged in Vivian's device to the broadcast tower. She's got a microphone and the spell book and – oh no! She's got hostages! She's tied them around the device to protect it!"

"We can't destroy the tech without hurting the people," Batgirl said. "If we can't take out the device, we have to take out Silver Banshee to stop the mind-control spell."

"It's a plan," Supergirl said.

The rising moon lit the roof of Shuster Tower. Silver Banshee crouched over the stolen spell book, tracing weird symbols on the page with her fingers. She murmured, "I will command. I will control. None will resist. First Metropolis. Then the world."

She looked at the full moon. In a language long forgotten, she began the incantation.

In the next second, Supergirl and Batgirl landed on the roof. Batgirl flung a Batarang. It knocked the microphone out of Silver Banshee's hand. The wraith-like crook snapped her gaze from the moon to the heroes.

"Again with the interruptions!" the Super-Villain hissed.

Supergirl blasted her heat vision. Silver Banshee easily dodged the searing attack and swatted away Batgirl's next Batarang with the spell book. She didn't even lose her page.

Batgirl winced. "Would you *please* show some respect for the book!"

Silver Banshee cackled. "You will show *me* respect!" Her mouth kept opening – wide, wider, wider still.

Time for a field test on these earpieces, thought Batgirl, bracing for impact. At such close range, if the two Super Heroes caught Silver Banshee's full wail . . .

But they heard nothing! The hacked earpieces worked! The girls could see Silver Banshee's unnaturally gaping mouth and the ripples in the air caused by the sound. But the wail had no effect on them.

Silver Banshee stopped her sonic strike. "Impossible," she muttered. She cleared her throat. She took in a huge breath and wailed again, with even more power.

No impact! Nothing!

Silver Banshee snarled at the pair. "What is this magic you wield that protects you from my wail?"

Batgirl grinned. "Not magic. Science. Like that tech you stole."

"And you're abusing both," added Supergirl. "Now, I think it's time for you to be quiet!"

Wail or no wail, Silver Banshee still had incredible super-speed and super-strength. Clenching the spell book to her chest, she launched herself at the Super Heroes.

OOOF!

Supergirl caught a knee to the stomach. She doubled over. But Silver Banshee turned away suddenly. Her attention was on Batgirl, who was sneaking towards the hostages.

With one hand, Silver Banshee tore up thick roof tiles and hurled them. Batgirl managed to handspring out of the path of the first tile, but not the second. It hit her in the back and knocked her off the roof!

"Batgirl!" Supergirl gasped.

Silver Banshee gave a wicked laugh as she spun around to face Supergirl. She lashed out with a kick.

Supergirl caught her foe's foot mid-strike. But before the hero could blink, Silver Banshee delivered an uppercut right on her chin!

Supergirl reeled up into the dark sky. For a moment, she eclipsed the full moon. Then . . .

CRASH!

The Girl of Steel landed on a rooftop several buildings away. She lay unconscious in the rubble.

Meanwhile, Batgirl plummeted from Shuster Tower. She wasn't panicking, though. It wasn't the first tall building she had been thrown off.

She grasped the edges of her wildly flapping cape to activate the glider mode. But the cape didn't respond! Batgirl turned to see that Silver Banshee's makeshift missile had ripped a hole in the fabric.

"Great," she said. "Plan B."

She whipped her grapnel gun from her Utility Belt and fired.

VVVVVVRRVRRRRRR

The line shot upwards.

CLINK!

The hook caught onto the roof ledge, several floors up.

JOLT!

Batgirl had stopped her fall! She hung safely against the side of the skyscraper.

Through a window, Batgirl saw a caretaker staring at her. He was frozen mid mop-stroke, his mouth hanging open. He raised a hand and gave a small wave.

Batgirl grinned and waved back. Then she activated the grapnel and was quickly reeled back up.

WHOOSH!

Batgirl sneaked onto the roof. Silver Banshee was again holding the microphone and muttering to the moon. Supergirl was nowhere in sight.

"Supergirl?" Batgirl whispered into her earpiece. No response. She was alone, at least for now.

Batgirl was immune to Silver Banshee's wail, but she didn't have any protection against the Super-Villain's fists. She couldn't fight the foe by herself. Her only chance to stop the mind-control spell from spreading over Metropolis was to disconnect the broadcast device. She crept towards the hostages.

As she closed in, one of the hostages began to stir. "Wha?" he said, groggy. Then he was suddenly alert and frightened. His words tumbled out. "What's going on? Where are we? Batgirl? What are you doing here?"

Batgirl winced at the sudden noise. "*Shhh*," she whispered. "I'm going to get you off this roof."

But it was too late. Silver Banshee had heard. She spun around, eyes full of anger, and let loose a wail. The hostage's head bobbed forward. He was out cold again.

What was the point of that? Batgirl wondered.

Then the Super Hero watched the path of the sonic blast. It rippled through the night sky and crashed right into a passing helicopter.

The pilot slumped as the scream knocked her out. The helicopter was now spiralling straight towards the streets of Metropolis!

Chapter 5

SONIC SPELL

Without hesitation, Batgirl leaped off the roof. She fired her grapnel at the skids of the out-of-control helicopter.

KLUNK!

It caught! As the chopper careened wildly, Batgirl swung at the end of the grapnel. Bit by bit, she reeled herself up. The spiralling made her as nauseous as Supergirl's super-speed.

"No time for that," she said, shaking it off as she moved towards the pilot.

In the cockpit, warning lights flashed and alarms beeped. "Yes, I know," Batgirl said. She lifted the pilot off the controls and wrestled to straighten the helicopter up.

HNNNNGH!

"Harder than it looks," Batgirl said between gritted teeth. She pulled back on the control stick as hard as she could. The helicopter's spinning was just starting to slow when–

CRRRASH!

The helicopter's tail hit the side of a dark building. Glass showered onto the street below. The tail rotor bent with a sickening metal scrape. No matter how hard Batgirl pulled on the control stick now, the chopper was going down!

"Supergirl? Are you there?" Batgirl yelled.

Through her earpiece, Batgirl heard Supergirl groan woozily. On the rooftop several buildings away from Shuster Tower, Supergirl was only semi-conscious.

"Still just me," said Batgirl. "Okay. I can do this."

She dropped the controls, unbuckled the pilot, held her around the waist, and then jumped from the helicopter. The two tumbled through the air, twisting and turning towards a building site. Batgirl unhooked her grapnel gun. She fired at the jib of a crane.

TWANG!

The line pulled taut as the hook caught. The two swung through the work area . . .

WHAM!

. . . and into a huge pile of sand.

It wasn't the softest landing, but they were both all right. Batgirl let out the breath she had been holding.

Then she caught sight of the smouldering helicopter. It was plummeting towards a crowded late-night street cafe. Batgirl jumped to her feet and rushed towards the impact zone. Maybe she could make it in time? She *had* to try. She ran, bracing for the helicopter to hit.

But it never did.

It stopped just above the pavement.

Batgirl saw Supergirl and let out a shout of joy. Supergirl had recovered! And she had caught the falling chopper! Supergirl grinned at Batgirl and gently lowered the helicopter to the ground. She used her super-breath to put out the fire on the damaged tail.

"Sorry I was late," the Girl of Steel said. She rubbed her chin. It still smarted from Silver Banshee's punch.

Batgirl launched at her with a huge hug. "I'm so happy you're okay!"

Supergirl hugged her back. "You too!"

WOO-HOO! YAY! YEAH!

The crowd by the cafe clapped and cheered for Supergirl. She gave a quick wave before turning to Batgirl.

"Back to it?" she asked.

"Ready as I'll ever be," replied Batgirl.

Supergirl grabbed her friend and was about to take off. Suddenly, the cheering crowd fell silent. Their hands dropped to their sides. Their eyes went glassy. Their faces went blank. As one, they turned to look towards the top of Shuster Tower.

"The spell is broadcasting!" said Supergirl. "But . . . it's not affecting us?"

"Silver Banshee's spell-casting voice must be on the same frequency as her wail," Batgirl realized. "Our modified earpieces are blocking the magic's effects." She looked around at the silent citizens. "It's definitely working on everyone else, though!"

"Then let's dethrone that scream queen!" said Supergirl. They launched upwards at super-speed.

On the roof of Shuster Tower, Silver Banshee stood surrounded by an eerie purple light. In one hand, she held the mic hooked up to the broadcast device. In the other, she gripped the ancient book. The Super-Villain's eyes glowed bright white. Her voice was low and spooky. She was deep into casting the spell, completely focused on the book.

"She's in a trance," said Batgirl. "Now's our chance!"

ZOOOM! Supergirl rushed to the hostages. She ripped the ropes away. The hostages were free! But although they were awake, they didn't move. They had the same blank expression as the people on the street below.

Meanwhile, Batgirl somersaulted across the rooftop, hurdled over ductwork and trampolined off an air-conditioning unit. In mid-air, she pulled out her grapnel and aimed.

TUNK!

The hook latched onto its target. Batgirl yanked the line, and the spell book flew out of Silver Banshee's hands. It fell to the ground, sucking in the weird purple light as its pages snapped shut.

Silver Banshee's eyes stopped glowing. She blinked a couple of times, remembering where she was. She saw the closed book. She screeched with rage, leaped forward and–

WHAM!

Supergirl sped over and landed a powerful punch square on Silver Banshee's chin. The crook crumpled onto the rooftop, foiled at last.

"That's right," said Supergirl. "You try being unconscious for a bit."

She bent two steel pipes to tie up Silver Banshee's hands and feet. Then she added one around the villain's mouth, just to be safe.

The hostages stirred. They blinked and shook their heads. "What happened?!" "Are you all right?" "Where are we?"

Batgirl helped them up, and Supergirl quickly checked the street far below with her super-sight. Everyone was back to normal. The spell was broken!

That kind of victory called for a high five.

SLAP!

While Batgirl called the situation in to Metropolis PD, Supergirl texted Vivian. She reported that the broadcasting device was unharmed and that the day was saved. "Couldn't have done it without you!" she added.

The scientist replied with a string of happy emojis – including a high five.

Batgirl crossed the roof and picked up the spell book. Only moments before, it had been glowing with menacing magic. Now it was once again simply a beautiful artefact.

Batgirl flipped through the pages. "Joan will be happy to see this again," she said as Supergirl walked up beside her. "Although, it might be safer to keep the book in the vault from now on. We should get it back to the museum."

Supergirl grinned. "I can finally see some fossils! Before we return anything, I'll need to borrow Superman's Phantom Zone Projector to lock up Silver Banshee," she said. "But I'm more than happy to close this chapter. It's been one wild night."

The teammates looked into the clear sky. The moon was bright and bold. Batgirl chuckled. "And you thought books weren't exciting!"

BIOGRAPHIES

AUTHOR

JAY ALBEE is the joint pen name for an LGBTQ+ couple called Jen Breach and J. Anthony. Between them they've done lots of jobs: archaeologist, illustrator, ticket taker and bagel baker. But now they write and draw all day long in their home in Philadelphia, USA.

ILLUSTRATOR

TEO DUARTE is an artist from São Paulo, Brazil. He first began working with comics as a teen while an assistant to Mozart Couto, a famous Brazilian artist. He never stopped working in illustration, and since then, his art has appeared in many children's books and comic projects, including *Tangled: The Series*.

GLOSSARY

banshee in Gaelic folklore, a female spirit whose scream is a sign that a person will soon die

broadcast send out sound and/or images through radio, television or the internet

compound area with many buildings that all belong to the same group

curator person who is in charge of an exhibit or subject area at a museum, zoo or similar place

grimoire book of magic spells

hostage someone or something taken and held until the taker gets what they want

incantation words said to do magic

neutralize make ineffective and unable to do harm

prototype first model of an invention, made to test the idea

trance state of being so focused that you are not aware of what is happening around you

wail long, loud cry or scream, often sounding as if it is done from sadness or pain

TALK ABOUT IT

1. At first, we don't know who or what attacked the Metropolis Museum. Were you surprised to learn later who was behind the attack?

2. Describe how Batgirl felt when she saw Supergirl grab the falling helicopter. Use examples from the text to support your answer.

3. Imagine if the Super Heroes hadn't got any help from Joan or Vivian. Do you think they still would have been able to stop Silver Banshee? Why or why not?

WRITE ABOUT IT

1. Batgirl and Supergirl work together to save the day. Write two paragraphs about a time when you teamed up with someone. What was hard about it? What was good?

2. Write a Justice League report on Silver Banshee. Describe how she looks, list her powers, and include any other info you think would be helpful to know.

3. Supergirl gets knocked out after rushing up to Silver Banshee in S.T.A.R. Labs. When the hero wakes, Batgirl is by her side. Write a chapter showing how Batgirl got there, and make it exciting!

READ THEM ALL!

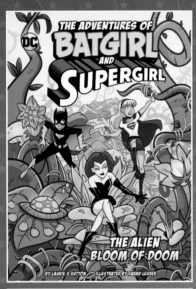